the Osbournes™

UN F***ING AUTHORIZED

The completely unauthorized and unofficial guide to everything Osbourne

Reed Tucker

BANTAM BOOKS

New York • Toronto • London • Sydney • Auckland

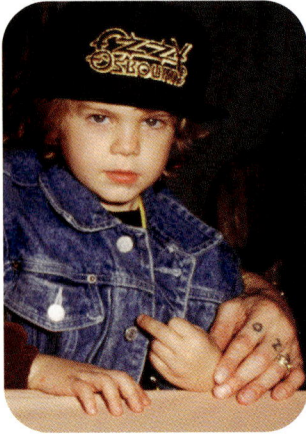

PHOTO CREDITS: Page 1: © Steve Granitz/Retna Ltd.; Page 2: © George Bodnar/Retna Ltd.; Page 3: © Scott Weiner/Retna Ltd.; Page 4: © Steve Granitz/Retna Ltd.; Page 5: © AFP/CORBIS; Page 6: © Mick Hutson/Redferns/Retna Ltd.; Page 7 top: © Andrew Kent/Retna Ltd., bottom: © James A. Steinfeldt/Shooting Star; Page 8: © Mitch Jenkins/Retna Ltd.; Page 9: © Neal Preston/Retna Ltd.; Page 10: © Sophie Olmsted Photography; Page 11 top left: © Gary Marshall/Shooting Star, top right: © John Spellman/Retna Ltd., bottom left: © Gilbert Flores/CelebrityPhoto.com, bottom right: © Paul Smith/Featureflash/Retna Ltd.; Page 12: © Sophie Olmsted Photography; Page 13 top: © Mick Hutson/Redferns/Retna Ltd., bottom: © Gilbert Flores/CelebrityPhoto.com; Page 14: © Sara De Boer/Retna Ltd.; Page 15 top: © Tammie Arroyo/AFF/Retna Ltd., middle: © Marko Shark/CORBIS, bottom: © John Spellman/Retna Ltd.; Page 16 top: © Mick Hutson/Redferns/Retna Ltd., bottom: © Sophie Olmsted Photography; Page 17: © Sophie Olmsted Photography; Page 18: © London Features; Page 19: © Bettmann/CORBIS; Page 20: © Sophie Olmsted Photography; Page 21: © Sophie Olmsted Photography; Page 22 top: © Bettmann/CORBIS, bottom: Jeffrey Mayer/Starfile; Page 24 top: © Bettmann/CORBIS, bottom: © Scott Weiner/Retna Ltd.; Page 25: © Miranda Shen/CelebrityPhoto.com; Page 26: © John Springer Collection/CORBIS; Page 27: © Tony Mottram/Retna Ltd.; Page 28: © Hulton-Deutsch Collection/CORBIS; Page 30: © Lynn Goldsmith/CORBIS; Page 31: © George Bodnar/Retna Ltd.; Page 32 top: © Bettmann/CORBIS, bottom: © Dennis Van Tine/London Features; Page 33: © Gary Marshall/Shooting Star; Page 34 top: Bettmann/CORBIS, bottom: © Steve Granitz/Retna Ltd.; Page 35: © Scott Weiner/Retna Ltd.; Page 36 top: © Jacques M. Chenet/CORBIS, bottom: © Gary Marshall/Shooting Star; Page 38: © Bettmann/CORBIS; Page 40 top: © Bettmann/CORBIS, bottom: © AFP/CORBIS; Page 42: © Bauer/Griffin/Shooting Star; Page 43: © Mick Hutson/Redferns/Retna Ltd.; Page 44: © Lynn McAfee/Retna Ltd.; Page 45: © Jen Lowery/London Features; Page 46: © Steve Granitz/Retna Ltd.; Page 47 top: © Mike Lynaugh/Retna Ltd., bottom: © Bergsaker Tore/CORBIS/SYGMA; Page 48: © Michael Montfort/Shooting Star

With special thanks to Marissa Walsh, Angela Carlino, Anke Steinecke, Rebecca Price, Raina Putter, Diana Blough, Diane Cain, Joanna Marutollo, Kathy Dunn, Andrew Smith, So Lin Wong, Audrey Sclater, Kim Soscie, Saho Fujii, Colleen Fellingham, Liney Li, Paul Aspesi, Alex Rudd, Janet Parker, Sandy Baker, Mike Wernig, Matt Walker, David Arnold, Bryan Tucker, Sandy Tucker, Lazlow Jones, Sarah Warnes, our enthusiastic sales force, and all the gang at the Random House warehouse.

This book has not been prepared, approved, licensed, or endorsed by MTV or any other person or entity involved in the creation or production of the TV program *The Osbournes*.

Back in Black: Kelly, Jack, Ozzy, and Aimee Osbourne at the 2000 Grammy Awards.

🦇 **"I'm not a musician,"**
Ozzy Osbourne once stated,
"I'm a ham." 🦇

F✱✱✱ING

Well, as *The Osbournes Un^authorized* will show you,
Ozzy is a ham *and* a musician *and* a whole lot more.
So, meet the Osbournes—the modern rock-age family!

F*****ING

Ozzy Osbourne

Real name: John Michael Osbourne

Age: 53

Birthday: December 3, 1948

Birthplace: Birmingham, England

Height: 5' 10"

Nicknames: Prince of Darkness, the Ozzman

Favorite band: the Beatles

Musical instruments he plays: harmonica

Most famous tattoo: *O-Z-Z-Y* across his fingers

Name of his first band: Approach

Animal heads he's bitten off: dove, bat

National monuments he's urinated on: the Alamo

Ozzy in his Black Salad—oops—Sabbath days . . .

He may be a rock legend to millions of fans, but to Aimee, Jack, and Kelly, he's just Dad. He snoozes on the couch, performs household chores, and occasionally horrifies them by walking around in just his underwear. Yep, Ozzy is pretty much like every other dad, only this dad puts bread on his family's table by rocking the faces off music lovers everywhere. Ozzy first hit it big in 1970 with his band Black Sabbath, a thunderously loud metal outfit that produced one of the greatest air guitar anthems of all time, "Paranoid." When he was kicked out of the band in 1978, Ozzy launched a solo career and quickly built a reputation as one of the wildest people in rock and roll. Two incidents in particular will probably follow Ozzy to the grave: In 1981, he accidentally bit the head off a live bat a fan had thrown onstage, mistaking the critter for a rubber toy. And as if one animal decapitation in his life weren't enough, a couple of years later in a meeting with record execs, he chomped on a dove that his wife had brought—ironically—as a peace offering to his label.

The press may have loved his hard living and sensational exploits, but by 1991, Ozzy had decided to clean up his act. In 1996, he founded the hardrockin' Ozzfest, a summer festival tour modeled after the successful Lollapalooza. Six years later the tour is still going strong. Ozzy's most recent album came out in 2001, and by 2002 he had evolved into a decent family man deserving of his own TV show.

When it comes to his kids, his parenting philosophy is to tell it like it is, citing examples from his own life of what not to do. So, kids: Stay away from doves.

. . . and as a solo artist.

Sharon Osbourne

Maiden name: Sharon Arden

Age: 50

Birthplace: London, England

Height: 5' 2"

Wedding anniversary: July 4, 1982

Favorite bands: Queen, Black Sabbath

Enjoys: shopping, cuddling with dog Minnie

Also managed: Smashing Pumpkins, Lita Ford, Coal Chamber, Quireboys, Gary Moore

She's not only Ozzy's wife but his manager as well. And has been for more than twenty years, ever since buying Ozzy's contract from her father, Don Arden, who managed Black Sabbath. In the Osbourne family, Sharon's the commander. No decision gets made, no trip gets planned, and no devil's head gets installed in the house without her approval. She's also got more marketing savvy than Don King and Madonna combined, and she's always

You may now bite the bride: Ozzy and Sharon on their wedding day in Hawaii.

controlled the business side of her husband's career, giving him time to focus on the creative side: spitting fake blood and throwing raw meat into concert audiences.

She may have been blessed with the brains in the family, but deep down, Sharon is still an Osbourne. "I can't sit here and say I'm the next Mother Teresa," she admits. And unlike other families where Dad is the disciplinarian, in this clan, it's Mom who lays down the law. While Dad is puttering around in his sweats or trying to figure out how to work the remote, Sharon keeps two teenagers and multiple pets in line.

F*****NG

Kelly Osbourne

Age: 17
Birthday: October 27, 1984
Favorite band: the Strokes
Ambitions: to move to New York City;
to avoid ever talking about sex with her father again
Enjoys: spending Dad's money, sulking
Celeb friends: Mandy Moore
Hair color at press time: pink

With her spiky hair, edgy wardrobe, and tattoo, Kelly's got the punk rock look down. And she's got the punk rock attitude to go with it. The Osbournes' oddball middle daughter is so morose, she makes the Prince of Darkness look downright cheery by comparison. With the exception of shopping, nothing ever seems to please poor Kelly. (Cheer up, you *are* living in Beverly Hills.) She spends most of her time on camera complaining about Jack, screaming during one of her patented freak-out episodes, or turning as pink as her hair from embarrassment whenever Dad talks about sex or

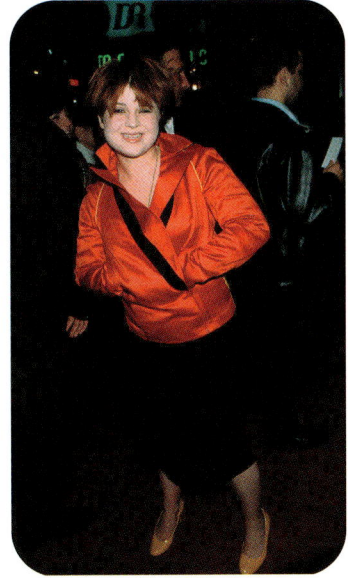

snogs Mom. She spends most of her time off-camera at movie premieres, parties, and awards shows. Maybe all that money Kelly's getting for season two will finally put a smile on her face.

KELLY, IT GIRL: clockwise from top left: *Glamour* Magazine's 2nd Annual "Don't" Party, 4/5/2002; *The Rookie* premiere in NYC, 3/26/2002; Clive Davis's pre-Grammy party, 2/25/02; Dad's Hollywood Walk of Fame ceremony, 4/12/02.

*F**ck**ING*

Fu**ing

Jack Osbourne

Age: 16
Birthday: November 8, 1985
Favorite band: Tool
Ambitions: to start his own record label;
not to get caught smoking pot by his parents again
Enjoys: guns, pissing off his sister
Celeb friends: Elijah Wood, pro skateboarder Jason Dill
Vision: less than 20/20

Jack is a "good boy" who does his old man proud by screwing up way less than Ozzy did at the same age—not that that's saying much. Jack calls himself an "ass-kicking fat kid" and can be found most nights tearing up L.A. nightclubs in search of the next great band. He works as a talent scout for Epic Records (hmmm, wonder how he landed that gig?), and music definitely seems to be his passion . . . because school certainly isn't. His job keeps him out so late, he sometimes has trouble making it out of bed and to school in the morning. Jack's got a black- and camo-heavy wardrobe and a classically dry British sense of humor. In a family of wiseasses, he's the biggest.

I WILL BE YOUR FATHER FIGURE:
Top: Alex P. Osbourne and Dad.
Bottom: "My dad's black magic is stronger than your black magic."

Aimee Osbourne

Age: 18
Birthday: September 2, 1983
Ambitions: to launch a career in music;
to avoid sitcom stardom at all costs
Rumored to be dating: Taylor Hanson,
middle brother of teen pop sensation Hanson

Reliable sightings of the elder Osbourne daughter are harder to come by than pictures of Bigfoot or of Prince Charles snogging Camilla Bowles. For whatever reason, Aimee decided not to take part in the series and never appears on camera. Not even for a cameo at Christmas. She lives in her own place nearby and has no interest in trading her privacy for a chance to have her face and name plastered on T-shirts, unauthorized books, and Osbourne commemorative mugs. The smartest of the bunch.

Extended Family

LOUIS OSBOURNE

Ozzy's elder son, from his first marriage. Much quieter than the other Osbournes (which, of course, isn't saying much), Louis can usually be found hanging around the house on major holidays.

Louis, Louis.

MELINDA VARGA

The household caretaker and nanny to Jack and Kelly . . . in theory. In reality, the young Osbournes chafe at having anyone watch over them, and Melinda and Jack frequently get into good-natured (but *f*-word-laced) battles. Melinda is Australian, perpetually happy, and one of the few people on earth who's able to understand everything Ozzy says. I wonder if she can understand former TV nanny Fran Drescher?

Fran "The Nanny" Drescher.

MIKE THE SECURITY GUARD

Mike, like Mr. T, pities the fool who tries to break into the Osbourne mansion. He watches over the perimeter of the house at night. In the Christmas episode, he's mistakenly arrested for breaking in while the family is away. He's soon back at work, though. He occasionally wastes some time watching TV with the family, and he's there to watch Ozzy's performance on *The Tonight Show*. But upon hearing the Ozzman's music, Mike looks like he'd rather be in jail.

I PITY THE FOOL: Mr. T.

Extended Extended Family

CRAZY BABY
A Japanese Chin. The dog used to be called New Baby, but the animal's neurotic behavior necessitated a name change.

MINNIE
A four-year-old Pomeranian. The undisputed queen of the house. "I want to break into song every time I see her!" Sharon exclaims. The fluffy pooch often goes on the road with the Osbournes.

LOLA
Jack's one-and-a-half-year-old chewing, vomiting, pooping bulldog. Almost single-handedly destroys the Osbournes' new house.

PIPI
A black Pomeranian co-owned by the elusive Aimee. The dog went missing for more than two months, prompting the Osbournes to offer a $500 reward (gee, guess they really wanted her back) in April 2002. With the help of *Live with Regis and Kelly* co-host Kelly Ripa, the dog was eventually returned.

The single life.

Still life with Japanese Chin.

MAGGIE
A brown-and-white Japanese Chin. Second in command, according to Sharon. Maggie, too, often travels with Minnie, Ozzy, Sharon, and the band.

LULU
A three-year-old Chihuahua that grunts a lot and looks like a seal.

PUSS
The Osbournes' sickly cat, which seems to especially enjoy the company of Kelly.

MARTIN BIANCO
A one-year-old Chihuahua that Sharon calls the "gay one."

Beverly Hills, 90666

RURAL PROGRAMMING: *The Beverly Hillbillies.*

Like Brandon, Dylan, Brenda, and the gang, the Osbournes enjoy the country's most prestigious zip code: 90210. Their Gothic mansion, located at 513 Doheny Road, lies in one of the plushest sections of America's poshest cities, Beverly Hills. The projects this isn't. "It's really nice," says Brian Sapir, who runs Happy Holiday Tours, a Los Angeles company that provides bus tours of celebrity homes. "It's quiet, and the streets are lined with palm trees."

Viewers of the TV show are already familiar with at least one of the Osbournes' neighbors (the annoying, singing pests next door who suffer Sharon's ham barrage), but who else lives nearby? Game-show king Merv Griffin has a home down the block, as does *Goodfellas* producer Irwin Winkler. Frank Sinatra, Clark Gable, *Star Trek* creator Gene Roddenberry, and George Burns also owned houses in the neighborhood before their deaths. Up the street is the famous Doheny Mansion (Ozzy is often seen walking the dog nearby), a gigantic Victorian house where dozens of movies have been filmed, like *The Bodyguard* and *Batman & Robin*. And if Ozzy ever wants to put out an elevator-music version of "Bloodbath in Paradise," he can head across the street, where classical guitarist Liona Boyd lives.

Before Ozzy and family moved into the grand, newly built house featured on the show, they lived in a more modest Spanish-style house just a few blocks away. "It was no biggie," says Sapir. So why the short move? Sapir says even before *The Osbournes* became a huge hit, the rocker's house was a

Opposite page:
STROLLIN' WITH THE DEVIL: Ozzy and Aimee.

Please please please let me get what I want.

popular destination for curious tourists. Because the Osbournes' previous abode didn't have a gate, some rabid fans would simply walk right up to the door and knock. Once, Ozzy answered, mistakenly thought a group of young tourists were friends of his daughter, and invited the strangers in. ("Attack, Minnie! Attack!") From then on, the family decided it needed a bit more security and had their new, heavily fortified home built nearby.

The Osbournes' posh new pad was wired with cameras to record every second of their lives before the family moved in, the twenty-fourth time they've moved. Viewers get a fly-on-the-wall perspective of most every room chez Osbourne as the family chats, fights, eats, bleeps, and enjoys various adventures involving ham.

On the first floor, you'll find a billiards-and-other-games room where Jack and Kelly like to hang out late at night with celebrity friends; an ornate, rarely used dining room; and a gigantic kitchen, which is where most of the action happens. Also on this floor, Ozzy's got his own room outfitted with a TV and home entertainment center so complicated it frequently sends Dad into fits of curse-laden mumbling. Back behind the house sits a large pool—which is probably required by law in this posh part of Beverly Hills.

Upstairs are Jack's messy bachelor pad, Kelly's pretty-in-pink bedroom, and Ozzy and Sharon's master bedroom—where, luckily, cameras are rarely allowed. There's also a home gym to keep those Osbourne waistlines in check.

This is the story . . . of 4 family members . . .

It's wild, it's wacky, it's Dan Quayle–approved! It's

The Osbournes—

reality TV like you've never seen it before. The half-hour cable show follows metal god Ozzy Osbourne and his family through their daily adventures. Ozzy; his wife, Sharon; and two of their children, Jack and Kelly (daughter Aimee declined to participate), are equal parts *Leave It to Beaver* and *The Addams Family*. They're creepy and they're kooky, and altogether kind of spooky, but in the end, they're basically just a normal (albeit foul-mouthed) family struggling to coexist in their spacious Beverly Hills mansion. The family also owns a hundred-acre farm in England, and there's a possibility the second season of the show will be filmed there.

The Osbournes premiered on MTV on March 5, 2002, and quickly became the highest-rated show on cable and in MTV history. Here's our take on the adventures of Ozzy and family. All aboard the crazy train!

F**KING

1 THERE GOES THE NEIGHBORHOOD
Introducing: Melinda the nanny
Original air date: March 5, 2002

The Addams Family.

The one where we meet those wacky Osbournes

A new chapter is beginning in the Osbourne family's life. They're moving into a new house and inviting millions of viewers to move in with them. While movers unpack boxes marked "Linens" and "Dead Things," tension builds among the family members. And not just the dubious, producer-manufactured variety found on other reality shows. These people are genuinely pissed off at each other, and damn, it's fun to watch. Eventually duty calls, and Ozzy, Sharon, and Kelly head off to Dad's performance on *The Tonight Show*.

Ozzytary

They're not the average American family, the show's intro claims, but if there's one thing this pilot episode makes clear, it's that the Osbournes are shockingly average. Take away the facts that they live in an enormous Beverly Hills mansion, drop *f*-bombs every other sentence, and have a creepy fondness for black nail polish, and they're pretty much like every American family ... who happens to be from England.

The elder Osbournes fight, they make up, they love, they stay up until the kids get in, they have trouble programming home electronics. And through it all, Sharon and Ozzy try to be the best parents they can be, battling to control their increasingly independent teenage children. Don't drink, don't take drugs, Ozzy advises Jack and Kelly before the kids head out, and he warns them to use a condom if they have sex. Fred MacMurray, eat your heart out.

In one of the episode's most revealing backstage moments, Jay Leno asks Ozzy to autograph a CD. Later, while stagehands cover their ears, Ozzy rocks the house, then returns home to watch his performance on the tube. Need more proof that we live in a media-obsessed culture? Here we are watching a show on TV about a man watching himself on TV. Figure that one out.

Ozz 'n' Ends

- Most memorable line: When asked if he's nervous about performing, Ozzy replies, "I don't need a laxative."
- Total curse words: 59
- Number of curse words the NBC censors fail to bleep during Ozzy's May appearance because they can't understand what he's saying: 1
- Prominent dis: Maybe he's more a Letterman guy. Sharon says Ozzy has reservations about doing *The Tonight Show* because "it's too mainstream."
- *Snap, snap: The Addams Family* premiered the same week as *The Munsters* in 1964 and ended the same month in 1966.

F**KING

2 BARK AT THE MOON
With guest stars Elijah and Hannah Wood
Original air date: March 12, 2002

My Three Sons.

The one where we meet the Osbournes' extended furry family

The Osbournes have pets. Man, do they have pets! And these animals are destroying the family's new house faster than Black Sabbath could trash a hotel room. They pee on rugs, poop on the floor, and treat furniture the way Mike Tyson treats an opponent's ear. These critters better shape up, if they know what's good for them. Remember what Daddy did to that bird. The worst offender is Jack's bulldog, Lola. Lola has defecated and chewed her way right onto Ozzy and Sharon's bad side, and the 'rents are seriously considering giving Lola away. Before they do, though, they do what everyone in L.A. does when they have a problem: They hire a therapist. But this pooch shrink seems

more full of crap than Lola and attempts to cure the dog of her bad behavior with a bunch of New Age-y bunk. Maybe the family should have hired someone with a rougher touch, like the Crocodile Hunter, Steve Irwin.

Make it stop, Daddy!

The Pink Ladies.

Ozzytary

It's surprising that the one who intervenes on Lola's behalf is none other than . . . Ozzy? Dad isn't exactly a card-carrying member of PETA. (In another reported bit of animal cruelty, an enraged Mr. Osbourne supposedly shot a bunch of chickens he kept in his backyard in the mid-1970s.) The fluffy and foofy pets seem more like Sharon's babies, and, frankly, there's hardly an animal a real man could be proud of among the bunch. It's hard to picture Clint Eastwood or Paul Bunyan owning a pretty Pomeranian. Nonetheless, Ozzy seems to generally enjoy the company of the animals—despite his constant bitching about their bathroom habits.

Ozz 'n' Ends

- Most memorable line: "Wanna know why my dog is dysfunctional?" Jack asks Sharon. "Because she's like me: angry at you."
- Total curse words: 73
- Cost to neuter a dog at a Beverly Hills animal clinic: $90
- Prominent plug: You're welcome, Eddie. Ozzy compares his critter-filled mansion to "Dr. Doolittle's house."
- Lola? Or Jack?: In Disney's *The Shaggy Dog* (1959), a boy turns into the neighbor's sheepdog. Fred MacMurray played the boy's father before starring on *My Three Sons* from 1960 to 1972.

3 FOR THE RECORD

Original air date: March 19, 2002

Does Father know best?

The one where Kelly has a strange birthday party

Ohhhhh, right. Before Ozzy became a gigantic sitcom star to rival Mr. Belvedere, he apparently made a bit of a name for himself in the music business. And this episode showcases Ozzy the musician, as the Ozzman takes a ride to a local record store, where legions of his Satanic-looking fans converge for autographs and photos. Later, Ozzy and Sharon's appearance on a radio sex-talk show pretty much guarantees Jack years of therapy and cold night sweats when the couple begins chatting about Ozzy's fondness for Viagra. Jack, listening outside, busts windshields for miles with his tormented screams. It's good to know that among children, some problems are universal.

Father Knows Best first debuted as a radio sitcom in 1949. The title ended with a question mark, suggesting that perhaps father did not *always* know best. When the series moved to television in 1954, where it ran until 1963, the question mark was dropped.

Winona forever

Ozzy has the letters *O-Z-Z-Y* tattooed on the knuckles of his left hand. He also has the word *thanks* on his left palm, *Mom* and *Pop* on his right forearm, and *Sharon* on his right upper arm.

Papa don't preach.

Ozzytary

As Ozzy continues working the publicity circuit in New York (Big up to P. Diddy!), Sharon is preparing for Kelly's birthday bash back home—a party so Goth it would make Marilyn Manson cringe. Whatever happened to a few balloons and a nice pony ride? Although she's only turning seventeen, Kelly reveals how grown up she can be when she shows Ozzy her new heart tattoo. And even though Dad's got more tattoos himself than a tattoo parlor's wall, he's not pleased. (Hmmm. Isn't this like Pam Anderson railing at her kids for getting implants or Michael Jackson punishing his kids for bringing home a monkey?) Ozzy later softens up. "It's not all that bad," he muses. "I thought she was gonna show me a picture of an eagle on her ass or something." Or worse: Justin Timberlake's name on her bicep.

Ozz 'n' Ends

- Most memorable line: Ozzy wondering about activities at Jack's hippie camp: "How the f✱✱✱ do you feed a tree? You put a f✱✱✱ing ham sandwich on the tree?"
- Total curse words: 35
- Cost to have a small tattoo removed: around $700
- Lucky charms for people born on October 27: poison ivy, lizards
- Prominent dis: Guess Ozzy didn't get his start in Menudo. He refuses to wear a jacket that makes him "look like Ricky Martin."

4

WON'T YOU BE MY NEIGHBOR?

Original air date: March 26, 2002

The Boonester.

The one with the ham

The feisty Brits next door blast techno music at all hours, host outdoor sing-alongs, and pretty much make life miserable for the Osbournes, in what truly has to go down as one of the most bizarre half hours on television not involving Farrah Fawcett. As the battle escalates and the neighbors hurl obscenities her way, Sharon decides to fight back by unleashing five pounds of pressed pork fury. Why exactly she feels that luncheon meat is likely to silence the rowdy bunch, we'll never know. Maybe she's hoping to give them a nasty case of trichinosis. When the big hunk of ham proves ineffective, the family decides to unload the nastiest, most horrible, most destructive weapon in their entire arsenal . . . the music of Black Sabbath. Meanwhile, viewers are treated to the Osbourne equivalent of *The Vagina Monologues* as Kelly bitches about her upcoming gynecologist appointment. (Hey, didn't we see this plotline in an episode of *Leave It to Beaver?*)

He lit up their life

Pat Boone, real name Charles Eugene Boone, claims to be a descendant of frontiersman Daniel Boone. He may be a good neighbor, but he hasn't had a Top 40 single since 1962.

Ozzytary

Who would have thought that in their ritzy Beverly Hills neighborhood, the Osbournes would be the quiet ones? Papa Osbourne may be the Prince of Darkness, but in this episode, it's his neighbors who are from Hell. If only some of the Osbournes were shirtless, this could be an episode of *Cops*. Things get so bad that the police show up and give the family a stern talking-to. If he weren't sacked out on the couch, Ozzy would probably be dying of rock star embarrassment. Jim Morrison got arrested for exposing himself. John Lennon got busted for dope. And the Osbourne clan nearly gets taken downtown for throwing bread.

But that isn't all. Ozzy, feeling Kelly's pain, gives her a speech definitely not coming to a middle school health class near you. It's moments like this that make *The Osbournes* so great: candid conversations between father and daughter. It's like they didn't even know the cameras were there.

Ozz 'n' Ends

- Most memorable line: Sharon tells the neighbors through the shrubs, "The big crosses, they're everywhere. We're very religious."
- Total curse words: 61
- Age at which Ozzy claims he first had sex: 12
- Punishment for vandalism proposed in California in 1996: paddling
- Prominent plug: His music may suck, but the Osbournes claim former neighbor Pat Boone was the best ever.
- But where's his body?: In 1990 Jim Morrison's graffiti-covered headstone was stolen from Paris's Père Lachaise cemetery.

PLAID TO THE BONE: *Roseanne.*

The one where Ozzy takes this show on the road

All that snacking Ozzy's been doing in previous episodes is apparently taking its toll. So to get ready for his upcoming tour, Dad decides he'd better get in shape and hits the fitness room with a strapping personal trainer. The Ozzman, Sharon, and Kelly hop aboard the Merry Mayhem tour bus, leaving Jack behind to work on his budding "record label." Ozzy arrives at the venue to check the sound and props. Or at least to see what Sharon has chosen for him. The arena has been transformed into a veritable winter wonderland, with freaky elves and a crucified Santa. Ozzy, though, is not at all happy with one effect. "Bubbles! Come on, Sharon. I'm f***ing Ozzy Osbourne, the f***ing Prince of Darkness," he whines.

Ozzy by the numbers

of children: 6

# of wives: 2

# of Grammy nominations as a solo artist: 1

# of Grammy wins as a solo artist: 1

# of tattoos: 17

# of tattoos daughter Kelly has: 1

# of Ozzy siblings: 5

# of dollars the first Black Sabbath album cost to record: 1200

# of dollars Ozzy donated to charity in 1992 for an earlier incident in which he urinated on the Alamo: 10,000

# of episodes of *The Osbournes* originally planned: 13

# of episodes aired: 10

# of ear-nose-throat doctors required backstage at Ozzy's concerts: 1

# of inches Ozzy is tall: 65

Ozzytary

If you've ever wondered who wears the black leather spiked pants in the Osbourne family, this episode leaves no doubt. Like her sitcom foremother, Roseanne, Sharon rules—and

Push it.

not just because Ozzy spends quite a while in a dress for a video shoot. Sharon controls the money (not to mention spending it like Elton John in a flower shop), and from the looks of things, manages just about everything else in Ozzy's life, from his tour itinerary to the price of a pair of Ozzy brand underwear. (Feel free to insert your own skivvy joke here.)

Never mind that the singer way back in 1992 announced that he was done hitting the road for good, claiming he wanted to spend more time with his family. (After watching the show, it's difficult to see why.) Not that it matters. Sharon's in charge here, and Ozzy's got less pull in this family than the Pomeranians.

Ozz 'n' Ends

- Most memorable line: Sharon drops the understatement of the year: "We're not the f***ing Partridge family."
- Total curse words: 50
- Percentage of California residents who are more than thirty pounds overweight: 15 to 19
- Price of a pair of Ozzy brand underwear: unknown
- Screen time for Ozzy's ass: 2 seconds
- Screen time for Aimee: 0 seconds
- We still think we love you: Only two members of the Partridge "Family" actually sang on the group's hit singles: teen heartthrob David Cassidy and stepmom Shirley Jones.

6 TROUBLE IN PARADISE

Original air date: April 9, 2002

JUST SAY NO: *Diff'rent Strokes'* "Very Special Episode."

The one where they have "the talk"

In sitcom terminology, this one's known as "A Very Special Episode." For one week, the fun-loving Osbournes forget about making rock music and cleaning up dog poo to have a serious chat about serious issues. This family proves it's got bigger problems than running out of Evian on the tour bus. It seems the Osbourne youngsters have been partying a bit too hard lately. Kelly is accused of slinking around town with a fake ID, while Jack's developed a bit of a liking for the Mary Jane. ("I learned it from you, Dad!")

SAY, SAY, SAY: Kelly, Jack, and Ozzy announce the lineup for Ozzfest 2002.

SHARON, CRUISE DIRECTOR: Warner Music's Grammy after-party 2002.

Ozzytary

Don't tell John Ashcroft or Tipper Gore, but as it turns out, Ozzy is a pretty decent father. Big Daddy, as he calls himself, can really lay down the law . . . when you're able to understand what the hell he's saying. "Don't do drugs," he tells the kids. "Look at me." Damn right. If the reality that it takes your father twenty minutes to put a new trash bag in the can doesn't scare you straight, nothing will.

So what's the kids' excuse for all their bad behavior? Kelly thinks it's because she and her brother have been brought up—how to put this politely—differently. You mean not every family says four-letter words at the dinner table, throws meat at their neighbors, and has a crew from MTV living with them? Regardless of their unique upbringing, could it be that the Osbourne kids are just a tad spoiled? Where's the episode where Ozzy tells Jack to get the hell outside and mow the lawn? When is Kelly gonna spend half a show cleaning the garage? Pardon, garages?

Ozz 'n' Ends

- Most memorable line: "Don't you think I know what it means when you order a pizza at f***ing twelve o'clock at night?" Ozzy asks Jack.
- Total curse words: 69
- Sitcom stars who have had substance-abuse problems: Matthew Perry, *Diff'rent Strokes'* Todd Bridges, Danny Bonaduce, Kelsey Grammer . . . we're running out of room.
- Surprise cameo: Rob Zombie, who's even scarier than Ozzy, shows up at the photo shoot.
- Pea soup: Ozzy once sat through eight showings of *The Exorcist*.

F***ING

7 GET STUFFED

Original air date: April 16, 2002

The Munsters was created by the same team who brought us *Leave It to Beaver.*

The one where the Brits get thankful

It's Thanksgiving at the Osbourne home, and as in many households around the country, it's a time for turkey, togetherness, and total dysfunction. But who could blame them? Thanksgiving isn't an official holiday over in Britain, so to these transplanted Brits, the whole idea is probably as foreign as driving on the right side of the road and a trip to the dentist. Still smarting from the leg fracture he suffered on tour, and fed up with Jack and Kelly's squabbling, Ozzy decides to pack up and head back out on the road. Sounds good, if you happen to be a rock star.

Hey, Ozzman, there's a Diet Coke on your head.

Ozzytary

Ozzy claims to be broken up about leaving his family behind—and he may be telling the truth, seeing as how his destination is the sunny metropolis of Grand Forks, North Dakota—but deep down inside, he must relish hanging out on tour with the band.

His retreat doesn't last long, however, as Sharon, Kelly, and Jack fly to Chicago to surprise him on his birthday, which Ozzy's lackey tells him he shares with Andy Williams. Now, if it had been Pat Boone, that would have been something. You gotta wonder, What the heck do you get Ozzy Osbourne for his birthday? Gummi bats? *The Munsters* on DVD? A blood transfusion? Fang implants? The real answer, as it turns out, is a jewel-encrusted pooper scooper. And a card addressed to the Prince of Darkness. Well, when you care enough to send the very best . . .

Oz Bless America.

Ozz 'n' Ends

- Most memorable line: You bite the head off one bat, and you have to live it down the rest of your life. Ozzy complains about his costume during a video shoot. "I'm sick to death of these f***ing bats."
- Total curse words: 49
- Ancient Egyptian name for the Prince of Darkness: Set
- Most ominous bit of foreshadowing: Sharon warns Ozzy not to step in the dog bowl.
- Prominent plug: He doesn't want his MTV. Ozzy watches the History Channel.

8 NO VAGRANCY

Original air date: April 23, 2002

The Cosby Show "jumped the shark."

The one with the annoying freeloader

Even multimillion-dollar Beverly Hills mansions have pests, and Ozzy has to contend with an annoying invader of his own: Jack's friend Jason Dill. Someone get the Raid. It's hard to pinpoint the exact moment when the family turns against him, but a good bet is when he melts a plastic chicken on the expensive griddle. In the meantime, Jack's bulldog, Lola, has dropped another load on the carpet and Ozzy's so mad, he's stammering. (Wait, that's how he always talks.) So unknown to Jack, Mom and Dad give the dog away. In the end, though, there's no more powerful relationship than the one between a boy and his dog and Lola is eventually reunited with her owner.

Dill continues his freeloading ways at the 2002 ESPN Sports & Music Awards.

Ozzytary

The Kato Kaelin wannabe claims he's a professional skateboarder, but his real talent seems to lie in scratching himself and belching. It's a classic sitcom ploy. As the season wears on, the audience begins to get bored with the expected gags from the normal cast (Look, Ozzy can't find a trash bag! Again!), so a feisty newcomer is introduced to shake things up. Remember Olivia from *The Cosby Show*? Or Cousin Oliver on *The Brady Bunch*? Scrappy Doo? Of course, new characters, for some reason, always end up being annoying, and Dill is no exception.

On the parenting front, Ozzy takes a backseat this time and allows Sharon to crack the long leather whip of discipline. When she finds a bottle of whiskey in Jack's room, what's Sharon's solution? She decides to pee in it to teach the boy a lesson—in a stunt that not only involves bad judgment, but, we're hoping, a funnel. The bottle ends up not belonging to Jack at all, but to Dill. The houseguest has seriously overstayed his welcome, and Sharon orders Jack to get rid of him by claiming that the family needs some "quiet time." Right, quiet time. Just us Osbournes, the giant crew from MTV, and those seven million viewers.

Ozz 'n' Ends

- Most memorable line: a wobbly Dill telling Jack, "Your mom respects my opinion."
- Total curse words: 57
- Most recent Kato Kaelin sighting: Moby's "We Are All Made of Stars" video
- Plastic chickens harmed during the making of this episode: 1
- Time it takes Ozzy to unwrap *Best of Chris Farley* DVD: 31 seconds
- Zoinks!: Shaggy is not a vegetarian. In various Scooby-Doo episodes he eats sardines, ham, hot dogs, beef jerky, salami, hamburger, anchovies, pepperoni, clams, liverwurst, meat loaf, and baloney.

F***ING
^

9 A VERY OZZY CHRISTMAS

Original air date: April 30, 2002

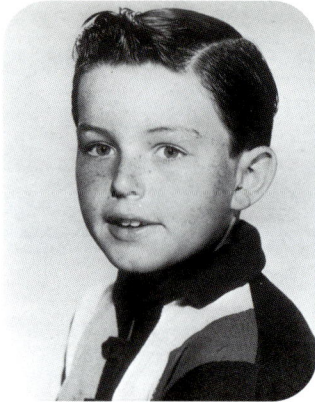

Leave It to Beaver, OK?

The one where the family gets in the holiday spirits

"I f***ing hate Christmas," complains Ozzy. This Xmas, Ozzy and nearly the entire family (*Paging Aimee . . . Aimee to the Osbourne family Christmas, please*) unwrap presents, then enjoy a lovely meal featuring gravy strained by Dad himself. Things quickly degenerate, and we suspect this may have something to do with the free-flowing champagne. Jack snaps at Kelly and soon the whole family is fighting and dropping enough curse words to make Santa cry. The only person who seems unaffected by all this chaos is Ozzy's son Louis. But then, Louis never really says much anyway.

Keepin' It Real

Take a look at some of the reality shows that influenced The Osbournes.

An American Family • PBS • 1973
This groundbreaking series chronicled seven months in the life of the Louds, an average California family. Once the cameras showed up, though, the parents' marriage disintegrated.

Real World • MTV • 1992–present
Throw one frat boy, one gay person, one struggling musician, one person of color, one naïve fresh-faced youngster, one all-American girl, and one freak (remember Puck?) together in a beautiful house furnished by IKEA and drama is bound to unfold.

Survivor • CBS • 2000–present
Backstabbing. Secret alliances. Public urination. Kind of like *The Osbournes*.

Making the Band • ABC • 2000–2001 • MTV • 2001–present
The good news: This series successfully combined music and reality television, paving the way for *The Osbournes*. The bad news: It gave us the band O-Town.

Project Greenlight • HBO • 2001–2002
This series about an amateur filmmaker making his first Hollywood film gave viewers a glimpse of the workaday lives of Ben Affleck and Matt Damon. And it showed that being a celebrity is, first and foremost, a job.

Ozzytary

Around the Osbourne household, it's not exactly a time for peace on earth and goodwill toward men. Or women. Sharon is using the holidays as an opportunity to make sizable charitable contributions to New York's many designer boutiques, Ozzy claims he's broke, and what would a sitcom Christmas episode be without a special Yuletide lesson? The one here isn't about the importance of generosity or the benefits of religion, but it's no less important: Don't f*** with knives, man! (a twenty-first-century version of "You'll shoot your eye out!" from the movie *A Christmas Story*.) Jack sets Ozzy and Sharon's parenting sense a-tingling when he gets a new pocketknife as a gift from a friend. (Is Eddie Haskell in the house?) Though Ozzy for once has no lesson from his own life about the danger of blades, he confiscates the knife from Jack and hides it in the fruit bowl—proving that his brain may not be so burnt after all.

Ozz 'n' Ends

- Most memorable line: In a touching Christmas moment, Ozzy and Sharon embrace. Then Ozzy whispers, "I adore you, sweetheart, now f*** off."
- Total curse words: 75
- Record high temperature on December 25 in Los Angeles: 85°F (in 1980)
- Prominent dis: Sharon and Kelly's complaint about Christina Aguilera's . . . ahem, "unusual" take on Christmas carols. "I wanted to abuse myself," cries Sharon.
- Prominent plug: Sharon buys enough Gucci to single-handedly pay for the CEO's Christmas bonus.

F*****ING

10 DINNER WITH OZZY
Original air date: May 7, 2002

THE NELSONS: Nelson, the musical twins of the long blond locks, are Ozzie's grandsons.

The one where Ozzy explains the family

Ozzy Osbourne, rocker. Ozzy Osbourne, dad. Ozzy Osbourne . . . philosopher. In this tenth and final episode of season one, the Ozzman gets downright pensive as he sups alone in his stately dining room, talks directly to the camera, muses about his existence, and lets slip that he's a big Beatles fan?! It was the Fab Four, he says, who got him interested in music.

The Original Ozzie

The Adventures of Ozzie and Harriet ran from 1952 to 1966. Ozzie and Harriet Nelson, real-life husband and wife, were one of the first TV couples to sleep in a double bed. We'll never know about Ozzy and Sharon.

Ozzytary

So what is the meaning of life for our rock-star-turned-America's-favorite-anti-dad? We're guessing the answer won't be found in tattoos or power chords. Or even in a Black Sabbath record played backward. No, after watching a whole season of the show, it seems clear that what's important to Ozzy is his family: Sharon, Kelly, Jack . . . and that other daughter, whatever her name is.

For *Osbournes* fans, this episode has to raise concerns—and not just because of that whole Jack-shoots-Kelly subplot. It appears that after just ten episodes (the series was originally slated to run for thirteen), the producers have run out of material. "Dinner with Ozzy," when you get right down to it, is basically just a clip show, that most odious of all sitcom devices, which cobbles together previously viewed scenes and leftover pieces of film and tries to pass itself off as a fresh episode. Was nothing new happening in the lives of those wacky Osbournes this particular week? Did Kelly not have any unusual doctor appointments? Did Jack not bayonet anything? Did Ozzy not at some point need to change the trash bag? Let's hope season two brings as much drama as the first nine episodes . . . or at least another scuffle with the next-door neighbors.

Ozz 'n' Ends

- Most memorable line: "People honestly think I live in a Bavarian castle, hanging upside down from a rafter with the rest of the bats," Ozzy explains.
- Total curse words: 58
- Animal heads bitten off during the making of this episode: 0
- Another creepy fan of the Beatles: Charles Manson
- Prominent dis: Ozzy says it's not so bad being him. "It could be worse. I could be Sting." Hey, his Police stuff was good.

Does *The Osbournes* seem weirdly familiar?

America's favorite hard-living group actually has a lot in common with classic sitcom families. Dick Van Dyke, Ozzie Nelson, Ozzy Osbourne? Darn right, says Ron Simon, television curator at the Museum of Television & Radio in New York City.

Q: The show is almost like a classic sitcom in a way, right?

A: Well, you're dealing with the nuclear family. You have the mother, father, and two kids. It echoes the 1950s and the problems that used to be part of *Father Knows Best* and *Ozzie and Harriet*.

Q: Are some of the plots the stuff of classic sitcoms too?

A: When Ozzy sits down with the children to teach them about drugs, that's sort of the classic "What did we learn today?" And the surprise party episode borrows more from *I Love Lucy*, where his family is throwing Ozzy a birthday dinner, and they're not sure how he's going to take it. It sort of reveals the tenderness beneath the family, and the episode ends like a formulaic comedy.

Q: How does the Ozzman compare to other sitcom dads?

A: Even though he calls himself the Prince of Darkness, Ozzy represents traditional values. He talks about growing up poor, and so he's got that traditional idea that you can work yourself up from nothing. It's something he believes in, and it's something almost every traditional dad believed in. And he tries to instill that same spirit in his kids. He relies on those traditional values, though everything else about him is nontraditional.

Q: Speaking of the kids, what sitcom characters do they remind you of?

A: It's funny with the kids. *The Osbournes* is sort of a reversal of where we are now with sitcoms, where the emphasis is more on the kids, on seeing life through their eyes. With this show the parents are the main characters. This is not *Malcolm in the Middle*. This is *Ozzy in the Middle*.

Goin' through the drive-thru with Dad.

Ozzy's Discography

Blizzard of Ozz (1980)
Ozzy's first solo album produced his most enduring hit, "Crazy Train."

Diary of a Madman (1981)
The little boy on the cover of this album is supposedly Ozzy's son Louis.

Speak of the Devil (1982)

Bark at the Moon (1983)

The Ultimate Sin (1986)

Tribute (1987)
This live album is a tribute to Ozzy's guitarist Randy Rhoads, who died in a plane crash while on tour in 1982.

No Rest for the Wicked (1988)

Just Say Ozzy (1990, live)

No More Tears (1991)

Live & Loud (1993, live)
Ozzy won his first Grammy in 1993 for Best Metal Performance with Vocal, for "I Don't Want to Change the World" from this live album.

Ozzmosis (1995)

The Ozzman Cometh (1997, greatest hits)

Down to Earth (2001)
The song "Dreamer" on Ozzy's latest was cowritten with Foreigner's Mick Jones.

F**king

"Sharon, ah dohn wahn tis gaddle frhh."

Pardon? Excuse me? With his garbled speech and heavy accent, Ozzy has more trouble communicating than the radio at a fast food drive-thru. Sam Chwat, director of New York Speech Improvement Services (www.nyspeech.com) and speech therapist to the stars, sheds some light on Ozzy's "unique" language.

Q: Can you understand what the heck this guy is saying?
A: Uh, most of the time.

Q: Does everyone from Birmingham, England, sound like this?
A: Well, Birmingham through a bottle.

Q: Do you think you'd be able to pull an Eliza Dolittle on Ozzy? From Brit street urchin to eloquent nobleman in seven easy lessons!
A: Well, in the best of all possible worlds, yes. But there's really no reason why he'd like to change. He's got a distinctive way of speaking, and no one will pay him to speak any differently. And he won't earn any more money for speaking differently, and certainly his respect quotient won't change if he speaks any differently.

Q: If you were insane enough to accept the challenge, how long would it take you to rehab his speech?
A: Oh, geez. I'd say it would take three or four weeks, give or take a few sedatives—for me.

Q: Does anyone else on the tube speak as unintelligibly as Ozzy?
A: No, I think he wins the prize. Ladies and gentlemen, we have a new category!

Ozzy's Filmography

Austin Powers in Goldmember (2002)—Himself

Ozzy filmed this cameo in the Osbournes' Beverly Hills mansion.

The Osbournes (TV series, 2002)—Himself

Duh.

Moulin Rouge (2001)—Green Fairy Vocal Effects (voice)

While pop tart Kylie Minogue played the Green Fairy, Ozzy provided the vocal effects.

We Sold Our Souls for Rock 'n' Roll (2001)—Himself

This documentary about Ozzfest 1999 by Penelope Spheeris, featuring Ozzy, Sharon, and Jack, premiered at the Sundance Film Festival.

Lemmy (2001)—Himself

Documentary filmmaker Peter Sempel's film about Motorhead's front man, Lemmy.

Little Nicky (2000)—Himself

Who better than Ozzy to be in a movie about the spawn of Satan?

Cribs (TV series, 2000)—Himself

The MTV show that started it all.

Private Parts (1997)—Himself

Based on Howard Stern's autobiography of the same name. The Osbourne family has also been on Stern's radio show.

South Park (TV series, 1998)—Himself (voice)

The "Chef Aid" episode. Not to be confused with Ozzy's performance at Live Aid in 1985.

In a Metal Mood (1996)—Himself

Those documentarians love the Ozzman!

The Jerky Boys (1995)—Band Manager

Guess Sharon was busy.

Parker Lewis Can't Lose (TV series, 1990)—Himself

The "Rent-A-Kube" episode. Our favorite.

The Decline of Western Civilization Part II: The Metal Years (1988)—Himself

This is your brain. Penelope Spheeris's documentary features Ozzy trying to fry an egg.

Trick or Treat (1986)—Reverend Aaron Gilstrom

Ozzy made his movie debut as an antirock (!) minister in this horror film. Watch out, Kevin Bacon!

REACH FOR THE STARS: Ozzy's 2002 Hollywood Walk of Fame ceremony.

F**KING
⌃

How do the Osbournes rate as a family?

For some insight, we asked Leora Lowenthal, a senior social worker at
New York University Hospitals Center who specializes in family counseling.

Q: Does peeing in a whiskey bottle qualify as good parenting?

A: You know, I don't think so. I'm not a fan of peeing in your children's beverages. I'm also not a fan of flashing your kids' friends. It's too provocative. Teenagers are too young to understand the goofiness in that. They're just like, "Oh, my God! Mom's boobs!" And Ozzy walking around in his underwear with things hanging out, that's just not good either. Kids should not be seeing that.

Q: None of us should. What do you make of all that cussing?

A: Truthfully, I don't feel so strongly about that. I think that cursing in and of itself is not something that would cause so much psycho-logical damage. Right now, though, to expect the kids not to curse, given the parents? It's sort of the same as Ozzy saying don't get a tattoo.

Q: Are the Osbournes better or worse than your average messed-up American family?

A: [Sighs] Well, I will say, for all of my issues with the Osbournes, I think there's a lot of ways in which they are good parents. The messages they give the kids about sex, about drugs, about being self-confident, and that it's okay to be different, I think that's great. In general, the kids do seem to have pretty good values. Given who Ozzy is, it would have been really hard for the kids to have a normal upbringing and not be aware of who he was.

Crazy Train

When the Prince of Darkness is singing for the queen of England, can the end of the world—or knighthood?—be far behind? Take a look at some of the other signs of the Osbourne family's amazing popularity—and the planet's impending doom.

May 6, 2002

Ozzy and Sharon attend the glitzy White House Correspondents' Dinner, a stuffy affair usually populated by senators, generals, and grumpy old journalists. The couple, who come as guests of newswoman Greta Van Susteren, are the talk of the dinner, and Ozzy twice jumps out of his seat to blow kisses to the adoring crowd. Even President Bush admits to being a fan of the Ozzman's music, and jokes, "Mom loves your stuff."

May 7, 2002

The Osbournes closes its first season as the most watched show on cable (and MTV's most popular show ever), dethroning WWE (formerly WWF) wrestling. Maybe viewers enjoy real fighting more.

May 9, 2002

Ozzy Osbourne, a man who has trouble putting a coherent sentence together, helps nab a $3 million deal for a pair of books.

June 3, 2002

The Ozzman performs alongside musical greats Paul McCartney and Aretha Franklin (and not-so-greats like Ricky Martin) at England's Golden Jubilee, a celebration of Queen Elizabeth's fifty years on the throne. If the seventy-six-year-old monarch's hearing wasn't fading before, it is now.

June 11, 2002

The *Osbourne Family Album* is released, featuring Kelly's cover of Madonna's "Papa Don't Preach" and former next-door neighbor Pat Boone's rendition of Ozzy's "Crazy Train." Couldn't they get the current next-door neighbors to perform their version of "My Girl"?

Reed Tucker has the letters *R-E-E-D* tattooed across the four fingers on his right hand. He is a graduate of the University of North Carolina at Chapel Hill. His work has appeared in *Time, Fortune, The New York Times, Newsweek,* and *Time Out New York*.

Reed Tucker lives in New York City.